BC # 93720

27537 EN
Mailbox Mania

Le
AT
Pc

THE CUL-DE-SAC KIDS

Mailbox Mania

Beverly Lewis

BETHANY HOUSE PUBLISHERS
MINNEAPOLIS, MINNESOTA 55438

Mailbox Mania
Copyright © 1996
Beverly Lewis

Cover illustration by Paul Turnbaugh
Story illustrations by Janet Huntington

Published by Bethany House Publishers
11400 Hampshire Avenue South
Bloomington, Minnesota 55438

Bethany House Publishers is a division of
Baker Publishing Group, Grand Rapids, Michigan.

Printed in the United States of America

ISBN   978-1-55661-729-4

Library of Congress Cataloging-in-Publication Data

Lewis, Beverly.
    Mailbox Mania / by Beverly Lewis.
        p. cm. — (The cul-de-sac kids ; 9)
    Summary: Fighting over a Fourth of July contest for the
best decorated mailbox threatens to tear apart the Cul-de-sac
Kids.

    [1. Contests—Fiction. 2. Friendship—Fiction. 3. Fourth
of July—Fiction.] I. Title. II. Series: Lewis, Beverly. Cul-de-
sac kids ; 9.
PZ7.L58464Mai   1996
[Fic]—dc20   96-4441
ISBN 1-55661-729-1 (pbk.)   CIP
                                                      AC

To
Kendra Verhage,
my talented young cousin.
Someday, I hope to see your
stories in print!

THE CUL-DE-SAC KIDS

ONE

Abby Hunter yawned and stretched. And yawned again.

Summer had come. Hot, fly-buzzin' summer.

No school. Nothing to do.

Abby missed school. She missed her favorite teacher, Miss Hershey. "Summer's boring," Abby said.

Abby's sister, Carly, crabbed about her paper dolls. "They're floppy," she said.

<u>Their</u> adopted Korean brothers,

Shawn and Jimmy, were tired of American rice. "It's too dry," they said.

All the Cul-de-sac Kids were bored.

Dunkum Mifflin boxed up his basketball. "Too hot to play," he said.

Stacy Henry was sick of sculpting. "The clay's too soft when it's hot outside," she said.

Jason Birchall fussed about his frog. "Croaker never says, 'Rib-bitt' anymore."

Eric Hagel complained about his paper route. "I never get to sleep in," he said.

But the Fourth of July was coming. The United States of America's birthday.

Abby and her friends stood in front of her house. "Four more days," she said. "I can't wait!"

Eric and Dunkum, Stacy and Shawn agreed.

The younger Cul-de-sac Kids looked at each other. Dee Dee, Carly, and Jimmy shrugged their shoulders. "We oughta have a club meeting," Dee Dee said.

"Good idea," Abby said. She was the president of the Cul-de-sac Kids. Nine kids who lived on one street.

Dunkum smiled. "Let's meet at my house."

Abby grinned. They *always* met at Dunkum's house. He had the biggest basement. "How soon?" asked Abby.

"Give me ten minutes to straighten things up," said Dunkum. And he jogged down the cul-de-sac.

Carly, Dee Dee, and the others crowded around Abby.

"Let's think up something to do," Jason said. "Something really fun!"

"Yeah," Eric said. "Let's brainstorm."

Stacy leaned on Abby's mailbox. "I can't think of anything fun."

Abby tried to dream up something.

Just then, a mail truck came down the street. Mr. Pete, the postal worker, stopped at each house. The kids watched

11

him till he came to Abby's house.

Mr. Pete waved to them. "Good morning, kids!"

The Cul-de-sac Kids waved, too.

Stacy backed away from the mailbox. Mr. Pete stuffed the Hunter mailbox full.

Abby stared at the mailbox. Then an idea hit. "I know!" she shouted. "I know what we can do!"

Carly spun around. "What?"

"Tell us!" Jason said.

Dee Dee's eyes got big. "Please?"

"Come on," Abby said. "It's time for our meeting. I'll tell you about it there."

And she raced down the cul-de-sac to Dunkum's.

TWO

Abby took off her sneakers. They were new. One red, one blue.

The kids lined up their sneakers along the wall.

Jason plopped down on the floor. The others did, too. "Okay," Jason said. "Let's get started."

Abby sat in the president's seat—a beanbag. "The meeting will come to order," she said. "Does anyone have old business?"

"Forget the old business," Jason

13

hollered. "Let's have the new stuff!"

"Tell us your idea, Abby!" Carly shouted. "We can't wait!"

Soon, all the Cul-de-sac Kids were shouting.

Dunkum whistled.

Quickly, they settled down.

"Now," Abby began. "Let's start over."

Eric's eyes shone. "Abby sounds like a teacher."

Abby grinned. She liked that. Maybe someday she'd be a teacher like Miss Hershey.

Jason swayed back and forth. He seemed wound up. "Forget school," he said. "Let's hear Abby's idea."

"Ya-hoo!" Dee Dee said.

Abby's voice grew soft. "I have a great Fourth-of-July idea."

The kids leaned forward, listening.

"A contest," she said. "We'll call it Mailbox Mania."

Eric yelled. "What's *that* mean?"

14

"Sh-h!" said Dee Dee. "Just listen."

"We'll decorate our mailboxes for America's birthday," Abby said. "With American themes. Whatever you want."

"How about Paul Revere's horse?" Jason stood up and trotted around.

The kids laughed. But Dunkum pulled him back down.

"Someone can judge our mailboxes," Abby said. "The best mailbox wins."

Jimmy raised his hand. "I judge! I good judge."

Abby smiled. "Maybe it should be a grown-up."

Dunkum suggested someone. "How about Mr. Tressler?"

"Let's take a vote," Abby said. "How many want Mr. Tressler to judge the mailbox contest?"

Hands flew up.

"Double dabble good," Abby said. "Mr. Tressler's the one."

Shawn stared at Abby. "Who will

decorate Hunter family mailbox? Four kids in Hunter family," he said in broken English.

"Good question," Abby said. "Any ideas?"

Eric raised his hand. "The four of you should work together. What's so hard about that?"

The rest of the kids agreed.

Abby glanced around. "Every Cul-de-sac Kid except Carly, Jimmy, Shawn, and me, is an only child. So the Hunter family will work together."

Shawn and Jimmy clapped. "Yip-p-e-ee!"

Carly frowned. "That's too many kids for *one* mailbox. Way too many!"

Abby hoped her sister was wrong about that. She hoped with all her heart.

THREE

After lunch, they got started planning. Abby and Shawn, Carly and Jimmy Hunter.

They sat in the backyard under a shade tree. They sipped on lemonade and played with Snow White, their dog.

Abby began, "How should we decorate our mailbox?"

None of them knew.

"Any ideas?" She waited for her sister and brothers to respond.

None of them did.

"Don't we want to win the contest?" she asked.

Carly pouted. "You're the president of the Cul-de-sac Kids, NOT the president of the Hunter family."

Now it was Abby's turn to frown. "Why'd you say *that*?"

Shawn shook his head. "This not working."

"Just a minute!" Abby snapped. "Remember what Eric said? We have to work together."

"Good luck," Carly muttered.

"Let's choose a theme for our mailbox," Abby said.

Shawn looked puzzled. "Like what?"

Abby thought. "The Statue of Liberty?"

"Too hard," Carly said.

"We can try," Shawn said. He smiled at Abby. "I will try."

Carly shook her head. "Dumb idea."

"Don't say dumb," Abby replied.

"You're not the boss!" Carly stomped across the lawn. She sat on the back porch step.

Jimmy climbed a tree. "No contest for Hunter kids," he said.

Snow White barked up at him.

Shawn told Jimmy to come down. He said it in Korean. Abby could tell he was mad. "We cannot plan this way," he said. He glared up at Jimmy.

"I stay up here," Jimmy shouted. "I not come down!"

Abby felt like a jitterbox. She reached for her notebook and pencil. And her lemonade. Then she stood up.

"Where you go?" Shawn asked her.

Abby brushed off her shorts. "Maybe you're right. This won't work."

"But we try . . . and try," Shawn replied.

Abby glanced toward the house. Carly was pouting on the porch.

Abby stared at the tree. Jimmy was

21

hanging upside down. "Looks like two against two," she said.

Shawn nodded. "We find a way," he said. "You see."

"I don't know." Abby sighed. "Maybe they should have Mailbox Mania without us."

Shawn's eyes were kind. "You say, 'Cul-de-sac Kids stick together,' well . . . Hunter family do, too."

Abby sat down in the grass. She wanted to feel good about Mailbox Mania. She really wanted to.

But how could she when her family was fighting?

FOUR

The next day, Abby got up early.

She read her Bible. And prayed. "Dear Lord, help Carly and Jimmy. They aren't trying very hard to win the contest. Help us work together. Amen."

At breakfast, Carly ate her pancakes with too much syrup. Even Mother noticed.

Jimmy slurped his milk. The sound bugged Abby. "Where are your manners?" she said.

"Where are yours?" he shot back.

"Children, please," said Abby's mother.

Shawn was the only quiet one. Abby wished she had just one brother and no sister. Jimmy and Carly could go fly a kite!

Abby and Shawn helped clean up the kitchen. Then Abby went to Stacy's house.

"Let's go swimming," Abby suggested.

"Can't," Stacy said. "I'm working on my mailbox."

"Oh, yeah. Lucky you!" Abby turned to go. She was heading home when Mr. Tressler came outside. He was swinging his cane as he walked.

"Hello there, missy," Mr. Tressler called to her.

Abby waved. She ran across the street. "Can I talk to you?"

He smiled his wrinkled smile. "You're talking, aren't you?"

Abby explained all about Mailbox Mania. "We need a judge," she said. "Someone who can be fair."

He leaned on his cane. "Hm-m, sounds interesting."

"Do you want the job?"

He rubbed his pointy chin. "What's the pay?"

"Very funny," Abby said.

Mr. Tressler's eyes twinkled. "I'd be honored, Abby. When's the big day?"

"The Fourth of July."

"I'll be there with bells on."

Abby wondered, *Bells on?* Then she saw his smile and knew what he meant. "Thank you!"

Mr. Tressler waved his cane.

Abby felt good about Mr. Tressler doing the judging. But she wondered about her own mailbox. Could she get Carly and Jimmy to work on it? Would it be done in time?

The contest was only three days away!

"Maybe Shawn and I'll decorate by ourselves," she said out loud. Excited, she rushed across the street—to her side of the cul-de-sac.

At that moment, Stacy came out of her house. She carried a shoebox full of paints, paper, glue, and scissors. An eager look spread across her face.

Abby waved to her. "Hi, Stacy!"

Stacy froze.

"What's wrong?" Abby asked.

Stacy hid the shoebox behind her back. "I . . . uh . . . I didn't want you to see this."

Abby frowned. "Why not?"

"Well, I—" Stacy stopped.

"What?" Abby had a weird feeling.

"You won't steal my idea, will you?" Stacy asked.

Abby held her breath. She didn't say a word.

"Well, you won't, will you?" Stacy said.

Abby folded her arms across her chest. "You know me better than that, Stacy Henry!"

And she ran home.

FIVE

That night, Abby couldn't sleep.
Crackity-boom! Early fireworks.

Something else kept her awake.
Starting tomorrow there were only two
days left. The Fourth of July—and Mailbox Mania—was coming fast!

It was late when Abby fell asleep. Her
dreams popped with the sounds outside.
In one dream, Jason was making popcorn in his mailbox. The hot sun beat
down.

Ka-bang! The mailbox exploded into

a giant popcorn ball.

Abby woke up. Caught in her covers. Too hot. She kicked them off and went back to sleep.

★　★　★

The next morning, Abby crept into Carly's room. Her closet door stood open. Carly was humming.

Inside the closet was a secret place. The sliding door led to a tiny space under the steps.

"Ps-s-t! Are you in there?" Abby called.

The humming stopped.

Rustle-rattle.

Then—"Keep out!" Carly shouted.

Abby caught a glimpse of Carly. She was working on something. Probably something for Mailbox Mania.

Abby inched closer. "What are you do-ing?"

Carly hid whatever she was making. "Go away!"

"We have to talk," Abby said.

"*I'm* not talking. And that's final."

Abby sighed. "I know what you're doing, and it's not fair. We have to work together."

"Nope," Carly said. "I'm making my own mailbox creation. And you can't stop me!"

Abby stared.

Carly pouted.

"Fine," Abby said at last. "We'll have Mailbox Mania without you." And she turned to go.

"Mommy!" Carly yelled.

Abby shook her head as she hurried outside. *Such a baby!* she thought.

Across the street, Eric was working on his mailbox.

Abby watched him from her front porch. It looked like he was using green clay. A clay sculpture!

She stood up for a better look. It was the Lady of the Lamp, all right. The Statue of Liberty!

Just then, Jason ran over to Eric. Abby could see what was happening. Jason and Eric were arguing.

"You copied my idea!" Jason hollered.

Eric shrugged his shoulders. "How was I supposed to know?"

"Well, I won't let you make it!" Jason shouted. He leaped toward the Lady of Liberty.

Abby gasped. "No!"

But it was too late. Eric's clay sculpture fell to the ground.

Abby felt sick. This wasn't Mailbox Mania at all! It was a Mailbox Mess!

SIX

Abby dashed across the street. "Let me help," she said.

Eric didn't say a word.

Abby could hear his short, quick breaths.

"What an awful thing," she said. "I can't believe Jason did this!"

Eric carried his clay pieces inside.

Next door, Mr. Tressler sat on his porch. His face looked very sad. As sad as Abby felt.

She stormed up to Jason's house.

Mrs. Birchall came to the door. Abby wanted to tell on Jason. But she didn't. "May I speak to Jason, please?"

Mrs. Birchall nodded. "I'll get him."

In a few minutes, she returned. Without Jason. "I'm sorry," she said. "I can't seem to find him."

Abby knew why. Jason was hiding!

"I'll talk to him later," she said. "Thank you." And down the cul-de-sac she ran—to Dunkum's.

Dunkum Mifflin would know what to do. He always did.

When she got there, Dee Dee Winters was ringing his doorbell. Her face looked like a prune. "I quit," she said.

"You what?"

"I'm quitting the mailbox contest," Dee Dee insisted.

Abby looked at the little girl. "What's wrong?"

"Everything."

Dunkum came to the door. "Hi," he said. "What's up?"

"You busy?" Dee Dee asked him.

"Kinda," he said.

"Don't tell me," she said. "You're working on your mailbox?"

Dunkum looked puzzled. "Isn't everyone?"

Dee Dee shook her head. "I'm not."

"Well, why not?" Dunkum smiled. "Need some help?"

"Now you're talking!" Dee Dee's face lit up.

Dunkum looked at Abby. "Is it okay? If I help her, I mean?"

"Don't ask me." Abby took two steps backward.

"You're the Cul-de-sac Kids' president, aren't you?" he said.

Abby studied Dee Dee. She *was* only seven. Then she thought of her sister— Dee Dee's best friend.

"What if Carly finds out?" Abby said.

"That might cause trouble."

"There already *is* trouble," Dunkum said.

Abby took two steps forward. "What do you mean?"

Dunkum's face twitched. "Maybe you should ask your sister."

"What's wrong with Carly?" Abby asked. But she already knew. Her own sister was making things hard. And horrible.

For everyone!

SEVEN

Abby called a meeting.

Stacy, Dunkum, and Shawn showed up.

"Where is everyone else?" Stacy asked.

Abby explained. "We have some problems. Carly and Jimmy are mad at me. Jason and Eric are fighting. And Dee Dee asked Dunkum for help."

"Why should Dee Dee get help?" Stacy asked.

"She's little, that's why," Dunkum said.

39

Stacy shook her head.

Abby was worried. Would Dunkum and Stacy start arguing, too? "What should we do?" she asked. "Do we need to vote about Dee Dee or what?"

Dunkum looked around. "There aren't enough members here."

Shawn agreed. "Only four kids."

"Well," Stacy huffed. "What's Dee Dee making that's so hard?"

Dunkum spoke up. "She's making an Abe Lincoln mailbox. With a top hat and beard."

"You're kidding," Stacy said. "She should've asked *me*! I'm the artist on the block."

"But *I* live closer," Dunkum insisted.

Stacy's eyes were tiny slits. "That doesn't mean anything!" She got up and hurried down the street—to Dee Dee's.

"Hey! Wait!" Dunkum called.

But Stacy kept going.

"Well," Abby said, "I guess that's the end of our meeting."

"Cul-de-sac Kids do *not* stick together. Not anymore," Shawn said. His eyes looked sad.

Dunkum left without saying goodbye.

Abby didn't know what to think. Were the Cul-de-sac Kids falling apart?

She sat on the swing next to Shawn. "Now what?"

"In Korea, we talk to wise people," Shawn said. "Older people—like grandfather or grandmother—are wise."

Abby thought of someone like that. "Maybe Mr. Tressler can help. He's old and wise!" She looked at Shawn. "You're a great brother!"

Shawn smiled. "Abby great sister . . . and friend."

Then Abby hurried to the house at the end of the cul-de-sac.

Could Mr. Tressler help?

Abby would find out soon enough!

EIGHT

Abby ran to Mr. Tressler's house.

The old gentleman was having a snooze.

He snored softly.

Abby crept up the porch steps and sat down. *I'll wait here till he wakes up*, she thought.

While she sat, she remembered happier days. Lots of happy days.

Not long ago, the Cul-de-sac Kids were getting along. They'd made Father's Day gifts. And had an Easter pet pa-

43

rade. They'd even solved a mystery—*The Crazy Christmas Angel Mystery*.

Best of all, they were true friends.

But something had gone wrong. Crazy-wrong.

Abby glanced over at Mr. Tressler. Could he help?

Snortle-choke!

Mr. Tressler awoke.

"I didn't mean to startle you," Abby said.

He'd slumped down in his chair. Slowly, he reached for his cane. He pushed himself up a bit.

"Are you okay?" Abby asked, getting up.

"Just a bit dazed," he admitted. "But now that you're here, I'm fine. Sit down, missy." He patted the chair next to him.

Abby smiled. Her friend had a charming way about him. He could turn problems into pudding—sometimes.

Abby didn't spring her questions on

him right away. She sat in the patio chair and chatted with him.

They talked about the sunny summer day. They listened to the *chirp-chip-chirping* of the robins. And they laughed together.

Soon, it was time for lunch.

Time had passed so quickly. Abby hadn't asked Mr. Tressler anything. Not one word about the fighting in the cul-de-sac.

"Abby!" her mother called from the porch.

Abby could see Shawn and Jimmy running toward her house. "Well, I better go," she said.

"That's a girl." Mr. Tressler nodded. "Never keep your mother waiting."

She started to say something else. But she spotted Dunkum chasing Stacy. More trouble!

Stacy carried long black strands of yarn in her hand. Dunkum ran after her wearing a stovepipe hat. Dee Dee was right behind them—yelling!

"What's *this* about?" Abby muttered.

Mr. Tressler leaned forward. "Dear me—trouble in the cul-de-sac?"

Abby shook her head. "This whole mailbox thing is a mistake!" She hurried down the steps and across the street.

Stacy sprinted across her lawn and into her house.

Dunkum didn't let that stop him. He ran right up Stacy's steps. He began to pound on the door!

Dee Dee grabbed Abby's arm and pulled on her. "Make them give me back my mailbox stuff!"

"Is that Abe Lincoln's beard and top hat?" Abby asked.

Dee Dee nodded. "Stacy and Dunkum are fighting. They're fighting over who's gonna help me."

Abby felt helpless. What could she do?

46

NINE

Abby stood there watching.

She wanted to drag Dunkum down off Stacy's steps. She wanted to shake him and tell him to stop.

Poor Dee Dee, she thought. *This is all my fault.*

"Can't you do something?" Dee Dee pleaded.

"I'm sorry," Abby said. "Not now. I have to go in for lunch." She headed across the yard.

"Abby!" yelled Dee Dee.

47

"Go ring Stacy's doorbell," Abby called. "Maybe she'll talk to *you*." Sadly, she headed home.

★   ★   ★

Abby could hardly eat.

Shawn and Jimmy sat across from each other at the table. They scowled.

Carly whined and refused to look at Abby. All through lunch.

Mother looked first at Abby, then the others. "What's going on with the four of you?"

Abby spoke up. "Everything's horrible. We're having a mailbox decorating contest. But nothing's working out."

Carly smirked. "*My* mailbox is ready."

Shawn shook his head. "We must make mailbox together. Four Hunter kids . . . together."

"Remember our meeting?" Abby said. "Remember what Eric said about working together? We're a family."

Carly poked out her bottom lip. "I wish we weren't!"

Mother's eyebrows bounced up. "Carly Anne Hunter!"

"Well, it's true!" Carly wailed. And she got up and stomped off.

Mrs. Hunter excused herself and left the table.

Shawn's eyes got big. Jimmy's too.

Abby felt like a jitterbox.

TEN

It was the day before the Fourth.

And the day before Mailbox Mania.

Abby sat under a tree in the front yard. She stared at their mailbox. It was all red and white now. Like a flag.

All the Hunter kids had decorated the mailbox. Mother's talk with Carly had changed things. Everything!

Abby was glad.

Next door, Stacy's mailbox was on display, too. It was blue with perfect white and red stars. And an American flag for the mailbox flag!

Abby tried not to look at Stacy's beautiful mailbox. But her eyes weren't helping.

Then Shawn and Jimmy brought the dog over. Snow White was panting. "She is very hot," Shawn said.

Jimmy just stood there. His eyes were blank.

Abby nodded. "I'm hot, too. But not from the heat." She shot a mean look at Jimmy.

"You are mad, yes?" Shawn said.

"Jimmy doesn't like our mailbox," Abby said. "I thought the fighting was over!"

When Jimmy heard that, he ran across the street. He sat on Eric's lawn and stared at them.

Abby wished she were an only child. Like Stacy and Eric. And all the other Cul-de-sac Kids.

★ ★ ★

When the mail came, Abby ran to get it. She reached for the letters. But there was something else inside.

A present. With a bright red bow.

"What's this?" she said.

Jimmy dashed over for a look. "Let me see." He peered inside.

"It's a present." Abby took it out.

Jimmy stood on tiptoes. "Is present for me?"

Abby looked at the card. "It's for you . . . and Carly, Shawn, and me."

Jimmy jumped up and down. "Yipp-ee!"

"Quick, let's find the others," Abby said.

"Open it!" Jimmy shouted.

Abby dashed into the house. "Carly!" she called. "There's a present for all of us in the mail!"

That brought her running.

Soon, the four of them were tearing the paper off. Abby opened the lid.

53

Shawn, Jimmy, and Carly leaned closer.

Abby held up the gift. "It's a puzzle piece."

"With words on it," Carly said.

Jimmy's face wrinkled up. "That not present."

Abby stared at the puzzle piece. "I can't see all the words. Something's missing."

Shawn and Carly each took a turn looking at the puzzle piece. "Who sent us this?" Carly asked.

"I don't know," Abby said. "It's a mystery."

Shawn laughed. "A mystery in the mailbox!"

Just then, the doorbell rang.

Carly ran to get it.

It was Stacy. "Look what I got in the mail." She held up a puzzle piece.

Abby studied it. "You got one, too?"

The doorbell rang again.

It was Eric and Jason this time.

54

"Someone put puzzle pieces in our mailboxes," Eric said.

Jason danced around when he saw Abby's piece. And Stacy's. "Hey! Maybe they fit together!"

The kids knelt down on the floor. Stacy and Eric moved their pieces around. They didn't fit Jason's piece. So they switched.

"Wait . . ." Abby laughed as Stacy's piece snapped into hers. "This is double dabble good!"

Carly giggled. "Let's see if Dunkum and Dee Dee got puzzles, too."

"Good idea," the kids said. They picked up their puzzle pieces and dashed out the front door.

ELEVEN

The Cul-de-sac Kids met Dunkum coming up the street. He was waving his present in the air.

Right there on the sidewalk, they tried to put the puzzle together.

"Look at that!" Abby said. "We're missing one piece."

Shawn tried to read the words. "It say something about us—the Cul-de-sac Kids!"

The kids leaned over the puzzle. Their heads almost touched.

"You're right," Abby said. She smiled at Carly. "Why don't you go find Dee Dee?"

Carly leaped up. "Okay!" She ran down the street to Dee Dee's house.

Zippo! Dee Dee flew out of her house. She checked her mailbox.

Abby and the others watched.

Dee Dee smiled when she spotted the present.

Carly was standing close by. She whispered in Dee Dee's ear and pointed to the other Cul-de-sac Kids.

Dee Dee let out a "Ya-hoo!" She scurried down Blossom Hill Lane. Toward them.

Abby and the rest of the kids circled around her.

Dee Dee looked at the unfinished puzzle and set her piece down. Right in the middle.

It fit!

"*Now* we can read it," said Abby.

58

The kids read out loud. "The Cul-de-sac Kids stick together."

They looked at one another. *Really* looked.

Abby smiled and gave Carly a hug. Then Jimmy came over and hugged Abby.

Soon everyone was hugging.

Except Jason. He was dancing! "We stick . . . stick . . . stick together," he sang the words.

"*Now* we do!" Abby said.

The kids cheered.

"Who gave us these puzzle presents?" Dunkum asked.

"I don't know," Dee Dee said.

"Me neither," Carly said. The two girls giggled.

Abby called a meeting right there on the spot. "The meeting will now come to order," she said. "Any old business?"

The kids grinned. "Forget the old stuff," they shouted.

Eric raised his hand. "We have a mystery to solve."

Stacy nodded. "We sure do!"

Abby called for a vote.

Nine hands flew up.

It was agreed—the Cul-de-sac Kids would play detectives.

"What about Mailbox Mania?" Dee Dee asked. "Aren't we having a contest?"

"That's tomorrow," Carly told her. "*Today* we have something else to do!"

Abby gathered up the puzzle pieces and stuck them in her pocket. She fell in step with Stacy and Eric. The others were close behind.

They were off to solve a mystery.

TWELVE

"Where do we start?" Jason asked.

Abby had an idea. "Let's talk to Mr. Pete, the postman. He might be up the street."

"Let's ride bikes and catch him!" Dunkum suggested.

The kids went home to get their bikes.

Mr. Pete was three streets up. He looked surprised when nine kids on nine bikes called and waved him down.

When he stopped, Dunkum and Abby

rode up to the mail truck.

"We need your help," Abby said.

"Something wrong?" he asked.

She explained about the presents.

"Why, yes, I delivered them today," said Mr. Pete.

Dunkum frowned. "But there weren't any stamps on them."

Mr. Pete nodded. "I noticed that, too."

Abby watched his eyes. Something wasn't quite right. She watched his mouth. Mr. Pete was almost smiling.

"How can presents show up in mail-boxes like that?" Abby asked.

Mr. Pete shook his head. "It's the strangest thing."

"Come on," Eric piped up. "*You* know how the post office works."

"I certainly do." Mr. Pete glanced at his watch. "And the U.S. Post Office wants the mail delivered on time. So if you'll excuse me . . ." And off he went.

Dunkum scratched his head. "I think he knows something."

"Maybe we should follow him," Jason said.

"We better stick close to home," Stacy said.

"We better stick together," Abby said, grinning.

They zoomed down the hill toward their cul-de-sac. And stopped in front of Dunkum's house.

"I'm starved," Jason said. "Let's have a picnic."

"Where?" Stacy asked.

"Mr. Tressler has the biggest yard," Abby said. "Besides, we haven't visited him much. Not all of us together."

"Good idea," Shawn said.

"Who wants to pack a lunch for Mr. Tressler?" Abby asked.

Nine hands went up. Abby voted too.

"Let's everyone bring something!" Dee Dee said.

And they did.

★ ★ ★

Mr. Tressler seemed to enjoy the company. He nodded and smiled when Abby sat next to him—beside the comfortable lawn chair.

After dessert, the kids showed him the puzzle pieces. Jason pushed through the circle and put the puzzle together. "Look at that," he bragged. "Five seconds flat!"

"Any second-grader can do that," Dee Dee teased.

Jason took the puzzle apart. He passed the pieces to Dee Dee. "OK, you'll be in second grade next year. Let's see how fast you are."

The kids watched her put the puzzle together. "The Cul-de-sac Kids stick together," they chanted when it was done.

Mr. Tressler leaned forward to look. "What a fine puzzle."

"Looks homemade," Abby said. "Don't you think so?"

Jason popped up. "We wanna find out who sent the pieces to us."

Carly giggled. "The mailman acted funny."

"You should've seen him," Dunkum said. "He was in a big hurry."

"I think he's keeping a secret," Eric said.

Mr. Tressler listened. Then he said, "What sort of secret?"

"We don't know yet," Abby said.

Mr. Tressler rubbed his chin. "Looks to me like you've got yourselves a mystery."

Stacy looked at her watch. "We can't spend all day solving it. Tomorrow is Mailbox Mania!"

Mr. Tressler sat up straight. "And I get to choose the best mailbox!" He tapped his cane on the ground.

Abby looked at Jimmy and Carly.

67

She looked at Shawn. "I don't know about the rest of you, but—" She paused.

Dunkum smiled. "I think I know what Abby's going to say."

"So do I," Carly said.

Mr. Tressler's face burst into a grin. "You don't need a judge? Is that it, missy?"

Abby nodded. "Maybe we should just have fun with Mailbox Mania. Without the contest." She looked around. "Let's vote on it."

The kids agreed.

"OK," she said. "How many for a mailbox contest?"

No hands.

"How many just for fun?"

Nine hands. No . . . ten. Jason raised two!

Eric pushed one of Jason's hands down. "Hey, no fair voting twice!"

Jason frowned and pushed his hand

back up. "I can if I want!"

"Whoa, there." Mr. Tressler raised his hand. "I thought the Cul-de-sac Kids stick together."

He turned and winked at Abby.

"Why . . . Mr. Tressler?" she exclaimed. "Do you know something we don't?"

"Let's have a look at that puzzle." He grinned at Abby and the others. "Five seconds, you say?"

Jason counted the seconds.

Mr. Tressler's bony fingers flew.

"Three seconds!" Jason shouted. "Mr. Tressler put the puzzle together in only *three* seconds!"

The kids cheered.

"Mr. Tressler made it!" Jason said. "*He* made the puzzle!"

"Thank you, Mr. Tressler," Abby said. "Thank you very much!"

Mr. Tressler's eyes twinkled.

The mystery was solved.

THE CUL-DE-SAC KIDS SERIES
Don't miss #10!

THE MUDHOLE MYSTERY

When Dunkum digs for buried treasure in Mr. Tressler's backyard, he uncovers a mystery—in a mudhole! The discovery turns out to be a muddy time capsule, buried many years ago.

Curious, the Cul-de-sac Kids sniff around for clues. Who buried the time capsule? Where are they now?

Dunkum and his friends are in for a big surprise!

ABOUT THE AUTHOR

Beverly Lewis remembers waiting for the mail as a kid. She wrote lots of letters to pen pals and other friends. (Still does!)

Beverly and her younger sister, Barbara, had lots of fun with their neighborhood friends. They made "Mushy Goo-Goo"—a secret recipe that included a little water and lots of dirt. They dressed their cats in doll clothes. They hitched up Maxie, their Eskimo Spitz, to a sled and went to the store in a blizzard.

They even had a carnival to raise money for a Jerry's Kids Telethon. And ended up in the newspaper, and later got to be on TV!

If you like books that tickle your funny bone, look for Beverly's next books in the Cul-de-sac Kids series.

Visit Beverly's Web site at *www.BeverlyLewis.com*.

Also by Beverly Lewis

The Beverly Lewis Amish Heritage Cookbook

GIRLS ONLY (GO!)†
Youth Fiction

Girls Only! Volume One
Girls Only! Volume Two

SUMMERHILL SECRETS‡
Youth Fiction

SummerHill Secrets Volume One
SummerHill Secrets Volume Two

HOLLY'S HEART
Youth Fiction

Best Friend, Worst Enemy   *Straight-A Teacher*
Secret Summer Dreams   *No Guys Pact*
Sealed With a Kiss   *Little White Lies*
The Trouble With Weddings   *Freshman Frenzy*
California Crazy   *Mystery Letters*
Second-Best Friend   *Eight Is Enough*
Good-Bye, Dressel Hills   *It's a Girl Thing*

ABRAM'S DAUGHTERS
Adult Fiction

The Covenant • *The Betrayal* • *The Sacrifice*
The Prodigal • *The Revelation*

ANNIE'S PEOPLE
Adult Fiction

The Preacher's Daughter • *The Englisher* • *The Brethren*

COURTSHIP OF NELLIE FISHER
Adult Fiction

The Parting • *The Forbidden* • *The Longing*

THE HERITAGE OF LANCASTER COUNTY
Adult Fiction

The Shunning • *The Confession* • *The Reckoning*

OTHER ADULT FICTION

The Postcard • *The Crossroad* • *The Redemption of Sarah Cain*
October Song • *Sanctuary** • *The Sunroom*

www.BeverlyLewis.com

*with David Lewis   †4 books in each volume   ‡5 books in each volume

From Bethany House Publishers

Series for Beginning Readers*

WATCH OUT FOR JOEL!
by Sigmund Brouwer

Seven-year-old Joel is always getting into scrapes—despite his older brother, Ricky, always being told, "Watch out for Joel!"

Series for Young Readers†

ASTROKIDS™
by Robert Elmer

Space scooters? Floating robots? Jupiter ice cream? Blast into the future for out-of-this-world, zero-gravity fun with the AstroKids on space station *CLEO-7*.

THE CUL-DE-SAC KIDS
by Beverly Lewis

Each story in this lighthearted series features the hilarious antics and predicaments of nine endearing boys and girls who live on Blossom Hill Lane.

JANETTE OKE'S ANIMAL FRIENDS
by Janette Oke

Endearing creatures from the farm, forest, and zoo discover their place in God's world through various struggles, mishaps, and adventures.

*(ages 6–8)   †(ages 7–10)

06C